This book belongs to:

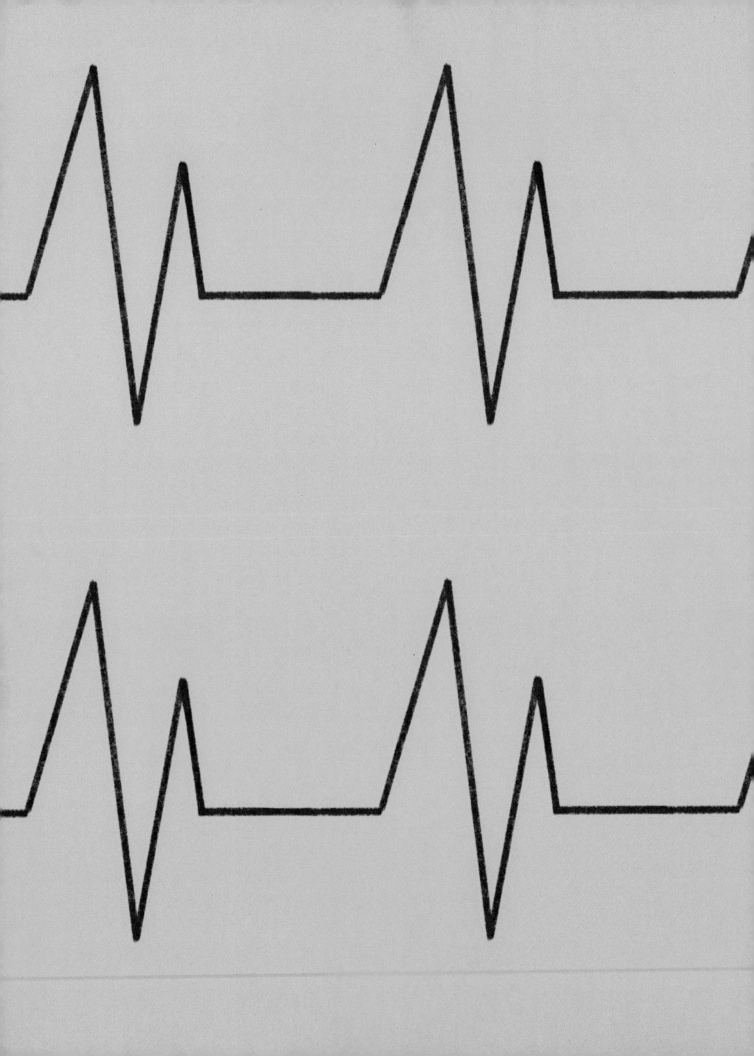

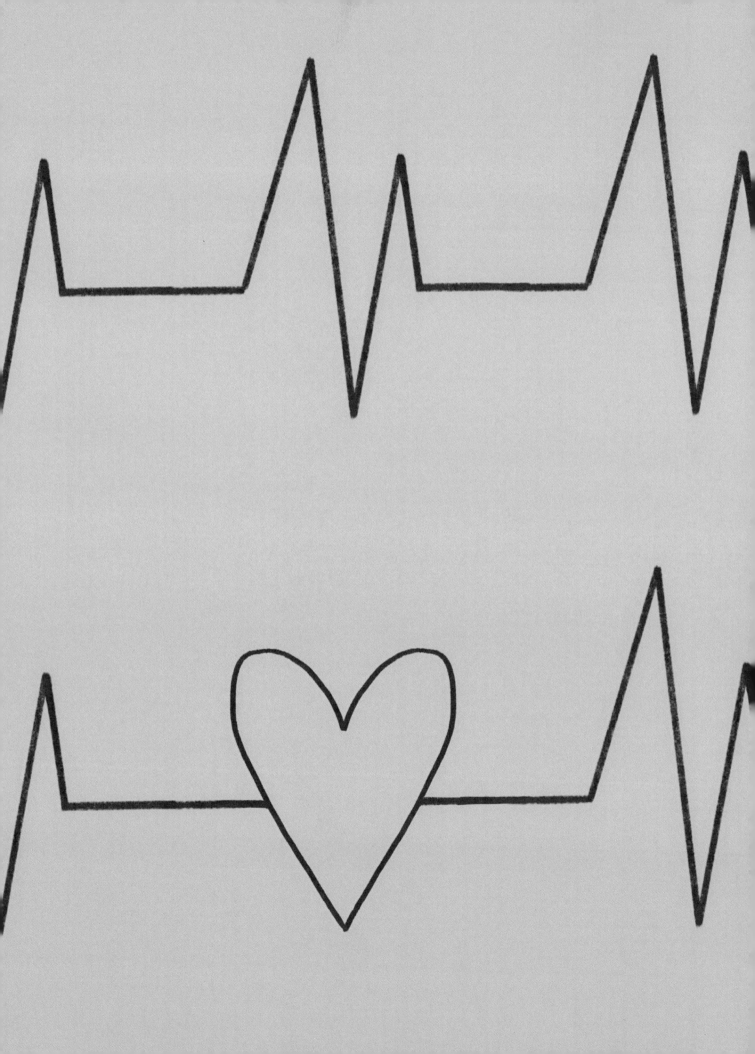

Dedicated to all the children that dare to dream—
You are brilliant and you will do great things!

Tamyra Donelson, Author

And to my Mom—
For being the best mom while working full-time in the
medical field. You make the world a better place!

Abbey Bryant, Illustrator

Meet the author,

TAMYRA DONELSON

Tamyra Donelson grew fond of storytelling at an early age, remembering the great stories her great grandfather, Finus Lee Douglass would share at the kitchen table, stories full of lessons that would feed her mind for centuries to come. Tamyra penned her first short story at the tender age of seven, competing in a young author's contest in which she did not place first–but she knew to stay persistent and knew her stories would touch the hearts of the world.

Serving as an K-8 educator for nearly 8 years, Tamyra noticed that some voices were not as precedent as others and aimed to share the rich experiences and lessons of the unheard.

Tamyra has a BA from the University of Illinois at Champaign Urbana and a M.ED. from the University of Las Vegas Nevada.

Tamyra is a Teach for America Alum— and the product of the many Chicago nonprofits that fuel and propel today's inner city youth and the Executive Director and Founder of the Kimberly L. Hollowell Nursing Foundation.

Look out for the next Finus Learning Center story!

First Printed Edition March 28, 2023
979-8-9878472-8-2

Written by Tamyra Donelson
Cover and illustrations by Abbey Bryant
Published by Finus Learning Center
Edited by Gina Caneva

KIMBERLY'S BIG DREAM

TAMYRA J.
DONELSON

ABBEY
BRYANT

"I will heal the world–You'll see!" said Kimmy.

"Ivy, did you have your fruit today?"
asked Kimmy.

"Not yet Kimmy Kim Kim!", teasing Ivy.

Kimmy thinks of the juicy jeweled
pomegranate seeds Mom prepares for snack.

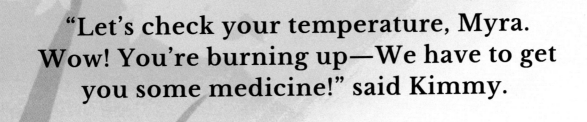

"Let's check your temperature, Myra.
Wow! You're burning up—We have to get
you some medicine!" said Kimmy.

"I can help, Elton!"

"Wait one second," said Kimmy.

"Momma, Elton is hurt but no worries—Nurse Kimmy is here to save the day!" said Kimmy.

"Let me help you, Kimmy," said Momma.

"Why thank you, Momma.
Let's go heal Elton," said Kimmy.

"Breathe—1–2–3,"
practiced Kimmy.

"Good job, Kimmy," said Momma.
"You did what great nurses do—
You helped Elton in his time of need."

Elton thanks Kimmy with a great big hug!

"Wow, I really did it!", said Kimmy.

"Yes, you did," said Momma.

"Not at the table, Nurse Kimmy," said grandma.

"Okay, Grandma —Myra,
I'll have to help you later,"
whispered Kimmy.

"Good night Kimmy—You did a great job helping your brother today. One day you'll be the greatest nurse ever," said Daddy.

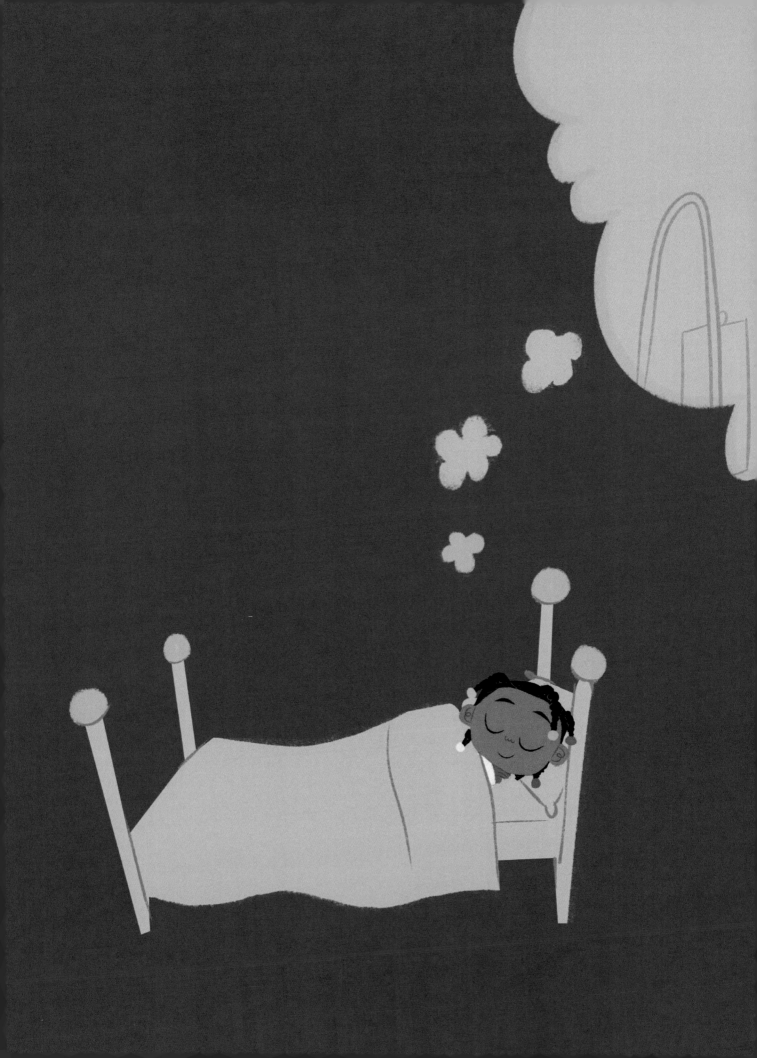

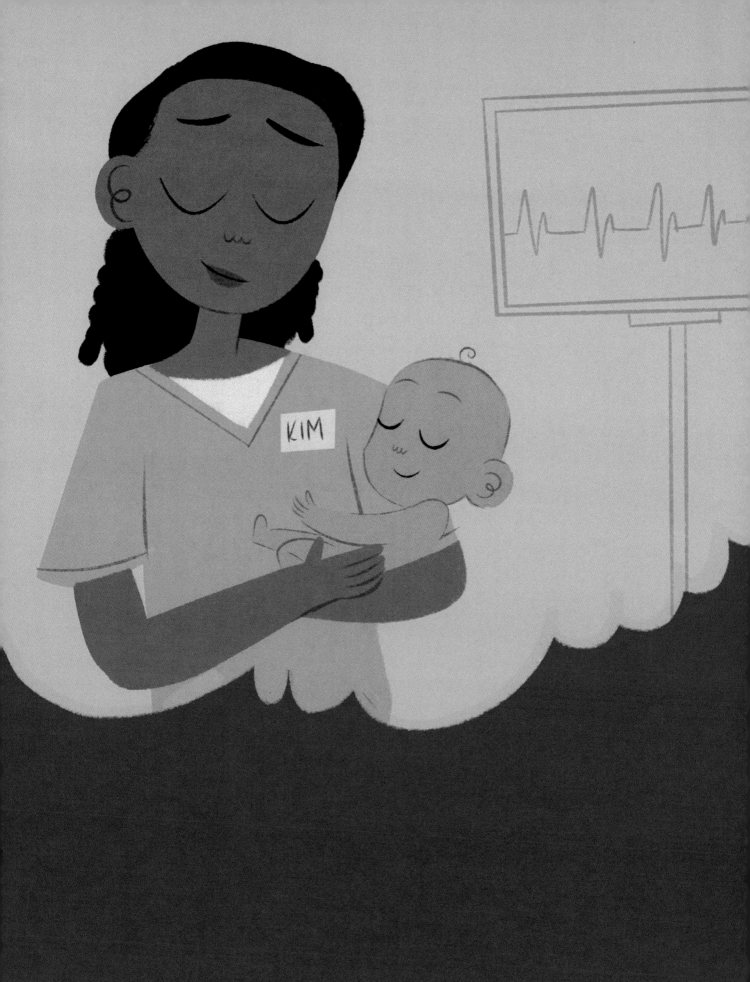

"When I grow up—I will be a NURSE. I will change the world and teach others how to be just like me!", said Kimmy.

"Kimmy, Yes you will. Yes you will,"
said her loving teacher, Ms. Flowers.

"Yes, I will," inspired Kimmy.

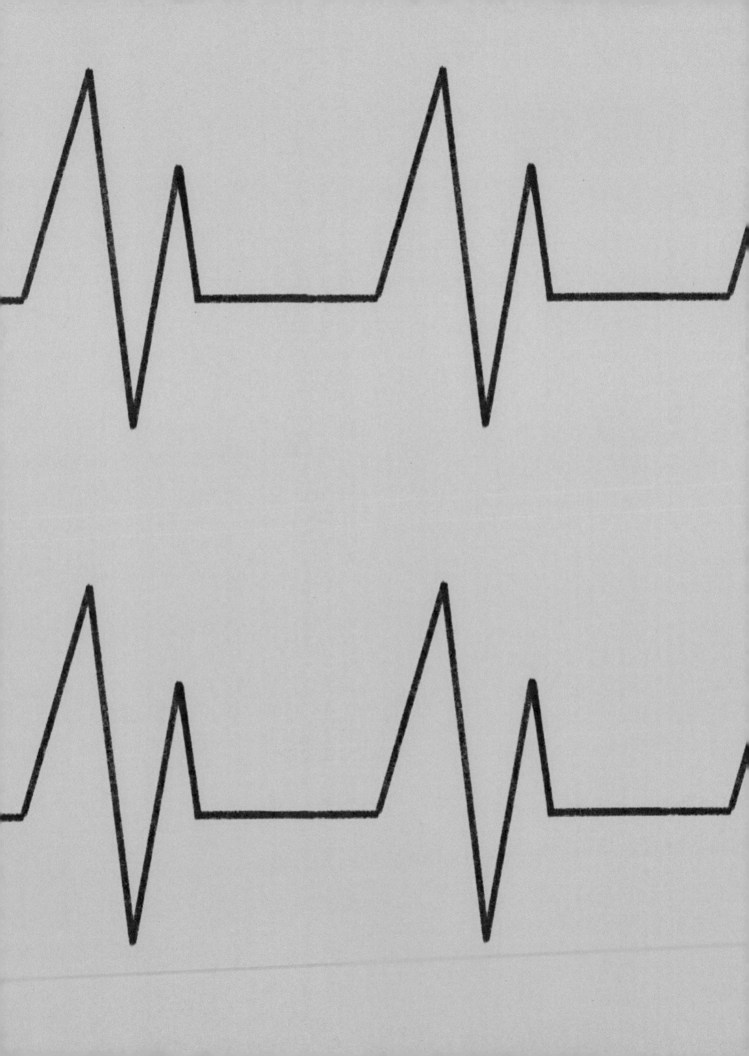

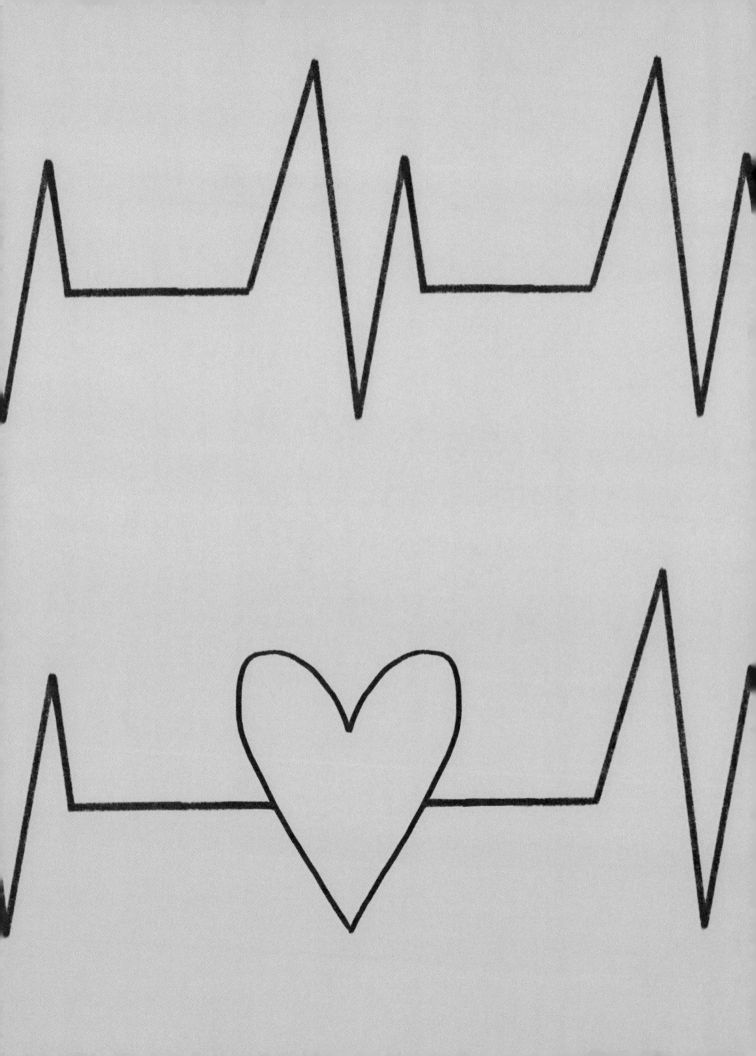

Made in the USA
Monee, IL
05 March 2023

29077688R00024